S0-AGX-854

The
Children on
Troublemaker Street

The Children on Troublemaker Street

Astrid Lindgren

illustrated by Ilon Wikland

Aladdin Books
Macmillan Publishing Company   New York
Maxwell Macmillan Canada   Toronto
Maxwell Macmillan International
New York   Oxford   Singapore   Sydney

First Aladdin Book edition 1991

Text copyright © 1964 by Macmillan Publishing Company

Illustrations copyright © 1964 by Macmillan Publishing Company

All rights reserved. No part of this book may be reproduced or transmitted
in any form or by any means, electronic or mechanical, including photocopying,
recording, or by any information storage and retrieval system, without permission
in writing from the Publisher.

Aladdin Books
Macmillan Publishing Company
866 Third Avenue
New York, NY 10022

Maxwell Macmillan Canada, Inc.
1200 Eglinton Avenue East
Suite 200
Don Mills, Ontario M3C 3N1

Macmillan Publishing Company is part of the
Maxwell Communication Group of Companies.

Printed in the United States of America

1   2   3   4   5   6   7   8   9   10

Library of Congress Cataloging-in-Publication Data
Lindgren, Astrid, 1907-
[Barnen på Bråkmakargatan. English]
The children on Troublemaker Street / by Astrid Lindgren ;
illustrated by Ilon Wikland. — 1st Aladdin Books ed.
p.   cm.
Translation of: Barnen på Bråkmakargatan.
Summary: Jonas, Maria, and Lotta, the rambunctious and
unpredictable Nyman children, have a year of roughhouse adventures
and prove that, while they are around, anything can happen.
ISBN 0-689-71515-3
[1. Brothers and sisters—Fiction.   2. Humorous stories.]
I. Wikland, Ilon, ill.   II. Title.
PZ7.L6585Cf   1991
[Fic]—dc20   91-15647   CIP   AC

Contents

Lotta Wants to Grow

Daddy says that before there were any children in the house, everything was peace and quiet. The noise started the minute Jonas was big enough to bang his rattle against the edge of the crib.

Jonas is my older brother. I am called Maria, and our little sister's name is Lotta.

1

Jonas made noise on Sunday mornings when Daddy wanted to sleep. Since then Jonas has been making more and more noise. Daddy calls him Big Noise. He calls me Little Noise. I'm not nearly so noisy as Jonas. Sometimes I'm quiet for hours at a time.

When we had another baby—it was Lotta. Daddy calls her Little Nut. I don't know why.

Mother calls us by our real names, Jonas, Maria, and Lotta. But sometimes she calls me Mia Maria—and so do Jonas and Lotta.

Our last name is Nyman. We all live in a yellow house on Troublemaker Street.

Right now, Lotta is furious because she isn't as big as the rest of us. Jonas and I are allowed to walk all the way down to the square by ourselves. But Lotta isn't.

Jonas and I go there every Saturday to buy candy from the storekeeper. But we always bring some back to Lotta, because we have to.

One Saturday last spring it rained so hard that it looked as if we would have to stay home. But

2

we took Daddy's big umbrella and went off just the same. At the market we bought jawbreakers and bubble gum. We sucked on the jawbreakers while we walked home under the umbrella. Lotta was watching from the window.

Poor Lotta! She wasn't even allowed out in the yard because it was raining so hard.

"Why does it always have to rain?" Lotta asked.

"So the vegetables can grow and we can have something to eat," Mother said.

"But why does it have to rain on the square?"
Jonas asked. "To make the candy grow?"

That made Mother laugh.

That night when we were in bed, Jonas said
to me:

"Mia Maria, when we go to visit our grandparents, we aren't going to plant carrots in our
vegetable patch. We're going to plant candy."

"Carrots are better for the teeth," I said. "We

4

can water them with my green watering can—the candy, I mean."

It made me happy to think about my little green watering can. It stands on a shelf in the cellar in my grandparents' house in the country. We always stay with them in the summertime.

You'll never guess what Lotta did when we were there last summer. Behind the barn is a big manure pile. Grandfather's helper, Mr. Johanson, takes the manure and spreads it on the fields to make things grow.

"What is manure good for?" Lotta asked.

Daddy told her, "Things grow better if it is spread on the soil."

"It has to rain, too," said Lotta. She remembered what Mother told Jonas when it rained so much that Saturday.

"That's right, Lotta." Daddy looked pleased.

That afternoon it started to rain very hard.

"Has anyone seen Lotta?" Daddy asked.

We all shook our heads. No one had seen her in a long while, so we started to look for her.

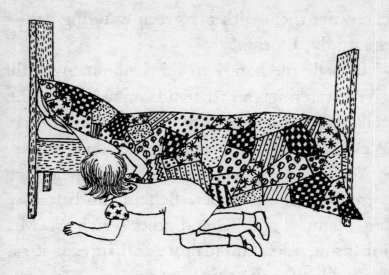

First we looked all over the house—in the closets, in the attic, in the cellar. But no Lotta.

Daddy got worried. He had promised Mother he would look after us. "She must be outdoors," he said.

We went out to the barn. We looked in all the corners and all through the hayloft. No Lotta.

Next we looked behind the barn. There she was—in the rain, sopping wet, standing right in the middle of the manure pile.

"What on earth are you doing there, Little Nut?" Daddy exclaimed.

"I want to grow and be as big as Jonas and Maria," Lotta said.

Sometimes Lotta can be very childish!

All We Do Is Play

Every day Jonas and I play games. We let Lotta play with us when we are playing games she knows.

But sometimes we play pirates and don't want Lotta to be with us. She's always in our way and keeps falling off the table, which is our ship.

8

Then she cries and she wants to keep right on playing anyway.

The other day Jonas and I were playing pirates and Lotta wouldn't leave us alone. So Jonas asked her:

"Don't you know what to *do* when you play pirates?"

"You stand on the table and jump and you are a pirate," Lotta said.

"But there is a much better way," Jonas told her. "You lie on the floor under your bed and you hold still."

"Why?" Lotta wanted to know.

"You just lie there pretending that you're a pirate and you keep on saying over and over, 'More food, more food, more food.' That's what pirates do," said Jonas.

Lotta believed this *is* what pirates do. She crawled under her bed and said, "More food, more food, more food," over and over again.

Jonas and I climbed up on our table and sailed away on the sea while Lotta stayed under

9

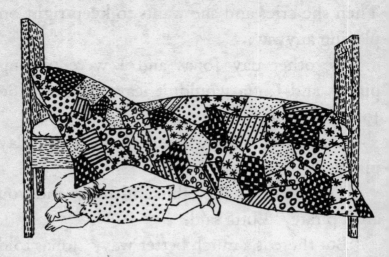

her bed saying, "More food." It was almost more fun watching Lotta than playing pirates.

"How long do pirates have to lie under the bed saying 'More food'?" Lotta asked at last.

"Until Christmas Eve," said Jonas.

Lotta crawled out from under her bed. "I don't want to be a pirate any more because I think they are stupid," she said.

Sometimes Lotta is a big help in our games. For instance, when we play angels—guardian angels, that is. Then we need someone to protect, so we protect Lotta. She lies in her bed

10

while we stand next to her moving our arms. We pretend that we're flapping our wings and flying and protecting her. But Lotta doesn't like that game much either. All she gets to do is lie still again. It's the same thing she does when she plays pirate, except that she lies *under* the bed then.

Sometimes we play hospital. Jonas is the doctor, I am the nurse, and Lotta is a sick child lying in her bed.

"But I don't want to lie in my bed," Lotta said the last time we asked her to be the sick child. "I want to be the doctor and stick a spoon into Mia Maria's throat."

"You can't be the doctor," Jonas said, "because you can't write a description."

"What can't I write?" Lotta asked.

"A description is what the doctor writes. It tells you how to take care of sick children," said Jonas.

Jonas can print and he hasn't even started school yet. He can read, too.

Jonas and I got Lotta to lie down in bed and be a sick child.

"How do you feel, my little girl?" Jonas asked. He sounded just like the doctor who visits us when we have the measles.

"More food, more food, more food," said Lotta. "I'm pretending I'm a pirate."

"Don't be stupid!" Jonas screamed. "Stop it. We won't let you play if you're going to be so silly."

12

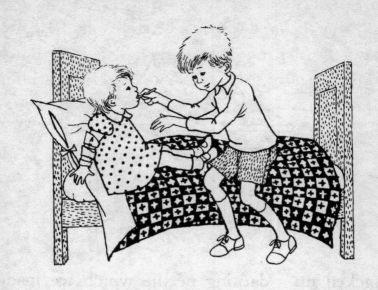

Lotta settled down and became a sick child again. She let us put a bandage on her arm, and Jonas held a big empty spool of thread against her chest. Through the hole in the spool he could hear that her chest was very sick. He stuck a spoon in her mouth. He could see that she was very sick there too.

"I have to give her a needle," he said. Once when Jonas was sick the doctor gave him a needle so he would get well again and that's why he wanted to give Lotta a needle. Jonas

picked up a darning needle which we made believe was the kind the doctor used.

But Lotta didn't want a needle. She kicked and screamed:

"Don't put a needle in me!"

"Oh, silly, we're only making believe," said Jonas. "I'm not really going to stick you, can't you understand that?"

"I still don't want a needle," Lotta howled.

That almost stopped us from playing hospital.

"Well, I'm going to write out a description

14

anyway," said Jonas. He sat down at the table and wrote with a crayon on a piece of paper. He printed it in block letters, but I still couldn't read it. This is how it looked:

SIK GIRL SHOUD HAV KARE. SIK GIRL SHOUD GIT NIDEL FRUM DOKTOR JONAS NYMAN

Jonas and I think it's fun to play hospital. But Lotta doesn't think so.

Lotta Is Stubborn

Our daddy is a very funny man. When he comes home from his office Jonas and I and Lotta meet him in the hall, and our daddy laughs and says, "Good heavens! How many children I have!"

Once when he came home we hid behind

the coat rack and were very quiet, and Daddy said to Mother, "Where's all the noise around here? Are my children sick?"

Then we jumped out from behind the coats laughing.

"You mustn't frighten me like that!" Daddy said. "There has to be a lot of crashing and banging when I come home, otherwise I get worried."

Once two trucks bumped together on the street right outside our house, and the crash was so loud that Lotta woke up from her nap. "What did Jonas do now?" she asked. Lotta thinks that Jonas makes all the noises in the world.

Lotta is so little and has such chubby legs that Jonas and I like to cuddle her. But she doesn't like that much.

There are lots of things Lotta doesn't like. Last week she had a cough, and Mother wanted her to take cough medicine. But Lotta just closed her mouth and shook her head.

"You're being very stupid," Jonas said.

"I'm not stupid," Lotta said.

"You're stupid because you won't take cough medicine," Jonas said. "When I take medicine, I make up my mind to take it and that's that."

"When I have to take medicine, I make up my mind *not* to take it and that's that," said Lotta.

She closed her mouth tight and shook her head. Mother patted her on the cheek.

"Well, then, my poor little Lotta, I guess you'll just have to lie there and cough."

"Good, and I won't have to sleep at all," said Lotta, happily.

You see, Lotta doesn't like to go to bed at night. Neither do I. But our mother has funny ideas! At night when we are wide awake she wants us to sleep and in the morning when we want to sleep she wants us to wake up!

Lotta should have taken that cough medicine after all, because the next day her nose was runnier than ever and she was coughing harder and harder. Mother told her that she couldn't go out. She asked me to go to the five-and-ten and pick up something for her. I ran all the way, and while I was standing there waiting for a clerk to come, Lotta walked in. Her nose was running worse than ever.

"Go home," I said.

"I won't," said Lotta. "I like the five-and-ten too."

She sniffled and sniffled, and finally a lady standing nearby said to her, "Don't you have a handkerchief?"

"Yes, but I don't lend it to strangers," was Lotta's answer.

Once, Mother took us to the dentist, Jonas and me and Lotta. Mother had noticed that Lotta had a small hole in one of her teeth. The dentist was going to fix it.

"If you are a very good girl at the dentist's, I'll give you a quarter," Mother promised Lotta.

Mother sat in the waiting room while we were with the dentist. First he looked at my teeth, but I didn't have any holes so I had to go back and wait with Mother in the waiting room. We sat for a long time waiting for Jonas and Lotta. Finally, Mother said:

"How strange, Lotta isn't screaming!"

After a while the door opened and Lotta came out.

"Have you been a brave girl?" Mother wanted to know.

"He pulled a tooth," Lotta said.

"And you didn't cry? My, what a brave girl you were!"

"No, I didn't cry," Lotta said.

"You are really a *very* good girl," Mother said. "Here is the quarter I promised you."

Lotta took the quarter and put it in her pocket. She looked very pleased.

"Let me see if it's bleeding," I asked.

21

Lotta opened her mouth wide, but I couldn't see any missing tooth.

"He didn't pull any tooth!" I said.

"Yes, he did . . . on Jonas," said Lotta.

Then Jonas came out with the dentist.

"I couldn't do a thing with your little girl there. She wouldn't open her mouth," said the dentist.

"We have to be ashamed of that kid everywhere," Jonas said as we were going home.

"But I hardly know him," said Lotta. "I won't open my mouth for people I don't know!"

Daddy says that Lotta is as stubborn as an old mule.

Mrs. Berg

Mrs. Berg is our next-door neighbor. Sometimes we go to visit her. There is a fence between her garden and ours. Jonas and I can climb over it. But Lotta can't. Mrs. Berg's dog, Scotty, has dug a hole under one of the boards, and Lotta crawls through there.

We had such a good time at Mrs. Berg's the other day. She has a bureau with lots of tiny drawers that are filled with interesting things.

"Please, Mrs. Berg, may we look at all those nice things," Jonas asked.

"Yes," said Mrs. Berg, and the first thing she showed us was a tiny doll that she had played with a long time ago when she was a child. The doll's name is Rosa.

Mrs. Berg is very old, but still not as old as Lotta thinks.

"Did you have Rosa with you in Noah's Ark?" Lotta asked her.

The night before, Daddy had been telling us all about Noah's Ark and how old man Noah had built himself a big boat that was called the Ark. Then it rained very hard for several weeks, and everyone who wasn't with Noah in the Ark drowned in the flood. It happened many thousands of years ago.

Mrs. Berg laughed and said, "But Lotta, dear, I wasn't in Noah's Ark!"

"How come you didn't drown, then?" Lotta asked.

Mrs. Berg showed us how she made one of the little drawers into a bed for Rosa. The mattress was a piece of soft pink cotton, and she had a piece of green satin for a quilt. She wore a blue dress.

In one of the other drawers I found a tiny glass basket with pink roses on it. "May we play with Rosa and the basket, Mrs. Berg?" I asked.

Mrs. Berg nodded Yes, and we hung the tiny glass basket on Rosa's arm and pretended that she was Little Red Riding Hood going to visit her grandmother with food and a bottle of fruit juice. On the piano was a bowl of chocolates. Some of the chocolates were shaped like tiny bottles and wrapped in tin foil.

We put one of them in Little Red Riding Hood's basket along with some raisins and almonds that Mrs. Berg gave us. Mrs. Berg's dog, Scotty, was the wolf. I was the grandmother, and Jonas was the hunter who comes and shoots the wolf.

"What about me?" cried Lotta. "Aren't you going to let me be *anything*?"

We let Lotta carry Rosa and the glass basket and say what Little Red Riding Hood was supposed to say. Rosa couldn't talk by herself, of course. But when Little Red Riding Hood

came up to Grandmother's house—which was
Mrs. Berg's living room—there were no more
raisins and almonds left in the glass basket.

"Where is the food for Grandmother?" Jonas
asked.

"Rosa ate it," said Lotta.

After that, Jonas didn't want Lotta to play
"Little Red Riding Hood" any more. And
Scotty was tired of pretending that he was eating Grandmother. Jonas held on to him, but he
wiggled around and finally got away. He
crawled under the sofa and every now and then

he would stick his head out and growl at us. Scotty doesn't like us to visit Mrs. Berg.

Then we looked at all the other things in Mrs. Berg's bureau. She has a pincushion of red satin shaped like a heart and a small picture in a gold frame of a beautiful angel with long white hair. That angel has two big wings and wears a white nightshirt. Lotta loves that picture, and so do I.

"But how did the angel get the nightshirt over its wings?" Lotta wanted to know.

"Maybe there's a zipper in the back of the shirt," Jonas said.

Mrs. Berg made waffles for us. She sometimes does when we come to visit her. "Since it's such a pretty spring day, I shall serve you waffles and hot chocolate in the garden," she said.

Mrs. Berg went into the kitchen, and we were alone in the living room. The two windows in the room were open because it was so warm. Jonas and I leaned out of a window, and Jonas threw me a marble that he had in his pocket.

I threw it back to him, and then we kept tossing it back and forth. But then I dropped it and it rolled down the lawn. Then Jonas thought we ought to see who could lean out the farthest. We each leaned as far out as we could and all of a sudden Jonas fell. I was scared. Mrs. Berg was scared too. She came running in just as Jonas went over the window sill.

"Jonas!" she cried.

Jonas was sitting on the lawn by this time. He had a big bump on his forehead.

"How in the world did this happen?" asked Mrs. Berg.

"Mia Maria and I wanted to see who could

lean out the farthest, and I won," Jonas said.

While Jonas and I were having our contest, Lotta had found Mrs. Berg's knitting lying on the sofa. Mrs. Berg knits sweaters and sells them to people. That naughty Lotta had pulled out the knitting needles and unraveled all of Mrs. Berg's knitting. She was sitting on the sofa all tangled up in yarn, and she was pulling and tugging at it.

"Lotta, what have you done?" cried Mrs. Berg.

"I'm making a sweater," Lotta said. "And, look, the yarn is all curly."

Then Mrs. Berg told us that we had better go out in the garden and eat our waffles, and after that we had better go home.

We sat in Mrs. Berg's garden drinking chocolate and eating lots of waffles with sugar. It was wonderful there in the sun with the sparrows hopping around us while we fed them crumbs.

Pretty soon Mrs. Berg said again that it was time for us to go home. Jonas and I climbed back over the fence, and Lotta crawled through the hole. We went to the kitchen to see what was for dinner.

"Fish," Mother said.

"It's a good thing we ate so many waffles," Jonas grumbled.

"So you've been to Mrs. Berg's?" Mother said. "Was she glad to see you?"

"Oh, yes," answered Jonas. "She was glad twice—first when we came and then when we left."

Mrs. Berg is the nicest person we know.

We Go on a Picnic

One day Daddy said, "On Sunday we're going on a picnic!"

"Whoopee!" Jonas and I shouted.

"Whoopee for the picnic!" cried Lotta.

Mother got up early on Sunday morning and made sandwiches and pancakes.

Mother also poured hot chocolate for us in one thermos and coffee in another for herself and Daddy. We were going to have soda pop, too.

Daddy drove the car up to the side door.

"Now, let's see if we can fit everything into this kiddy car," he said. "How in the world are we going to make room for Mother, Big Noise, Little Noise, Little Nut, twenty-six pancakes, and I don't know how many sandwiches?"

"And Bamsie," said Lotta.

Bamsie is a big pink cloth pig that Lotta drags around with her everywhere. She thinks he is a bear and so she calls him Bamsie Bear.

"He's a pig and he always has been!" Jonas always tells her.

Then Lotta cries and says that Bamsie is too a bear.

"Bears aren't pink," Jonas teases. "By the way, Lotta, is it a polar bear or a regular bear?"

"It's a piggly bear," says Lotta.

Lotta wanted her piggly bear to come with

34

us on the picnic. When we were all packed into the car, she asked:

"Mother, can pigs have children?"

"Do you mean Bamsie or do you mean real pigs like the ones in the country?" Mother asked.

Lotta said that she meant real live pigs and not bears like Bamsie. Mother said that of course real live pigs could have children.

"Of course they can't," said Jonas.

"But you know they can," Mother said.

"It's impossible for them to have *children*," Jonas said. "They can only have *little pigs*."

We all laughed, and Daddy said that Big Noise, Little Noise, and Little Nut were the cleverest people he'd ever met.

Daddy kept on driving until we came to a small lake. Then he parked the car on a dirt road in the woods and we all helped carry the picnic things down to the lake.

A long wharf went out into the water, and Jonas and Lotta wanted to go out to the end of

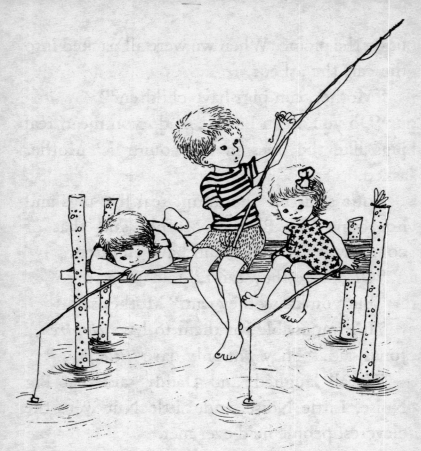

it to see if there were any fish. Mother settled
down in the grass and said to Daddy, "I'm going
to lie here all day and not move. You can take
care of the kids."

Daddy came with us to the end of the wharf.
We lay down on our stomachs and watched lots

of tiny fish swimming around very fast. Daddy got some long sticks from the woods and made fishing rods for us. He tied strings on them and put needles on the ends for hooks. We used breadcrumbs for bait and sat there fishing for a long time. But we didn't get a single nibble.

Next we went walking in the woods. Mother warned us not to go too far.

We saw a bird fly into a bush and then fly away again. We went over to look closer and there among the branches, almost on the ground, was a bird's nest with four tiny blue eggs in it! They were the cutest eggs I've ever seen. Lotta wanted to stay there looking at the bird's nest. She held Bamsie up so he could have a look too. But Jonas and I saw a good tree to climb and we made Lotta come along with us.

I'm not afraid of climbing trees and neither is Jonas, but Lotta is. We had to help her climb up part of the way. Then she started to scream:

"Let me down, let me down!"

When she got down she looked up angrily

at the tree and said, "Only crazy people climb trees like this!"

Before we could climb up any farther, Mother called us to come and eat, so we ran back to the lake. Mother had spread a cloth on the grass. She laid out the sandwiches and pancakes and all the rest. She had even put yellow buttercups in a glass for a centerpiece.

We all sat around in the grass enjoying the picnic and thinking how much more fun it was

here than eating around the dining-room table.
The pancakes were delicious because we put
jam and sugar on them. The sandwiches were
good, too. I liked the roast beef best, but Jonas
liked the egg and anchovy, so we traded. Lotta
liked all kinds best so she wouldn't trade with
anybody. Lotta is always hungry. She's refused
to eat only once in her whole life and that was
because she was sick. Mother was very worried
when Lotta wouldn't eat. One night when she
was saying her prayers, she said:

"And, dear God, make me want to eat again
—but not salmon patties!"

Lotta, Jonas, and I each got a bottle of soda pop. Lotta went down to the beach for some sand to put in her soda, and when we asked her why she did that she said, "I only want to find out how it tastes."

After lunch Daddy stretched out in the grass. "The sun feels so good I think I'll take a nap," he said. "You children will have to take care of yourselves for a while. But remember, you're not allowed out on the boat landing!"

We didn't go on the boat landing. But a little farther down the lake there was a big rock. We climbed up on it because Jonas wanted to show us how Daddy dives.

"He does like this," said Jonas, stretching his arms up in the air, and jumping.

Before we knew it, Jonas had landed in the water. He didn't mean to. And to make things worse, Mother had said we weren't allowed in the water because it was too cold. But he went down in the lake like a stone. Lotta and I screamed. I grabbed a long stick that was lying

on the rock, and when Jonas came up again, he grabbed hold of it. Lotta just stood there laughing. Daddy and Mother came running, and Daddy hauled Jonas up out of the water.

"Jonas, what on earth did you do?" asked Mother.

"He was only going to show us what Daddy does when he dives," said Lotta. And then she laughed again, because she thought Jonas' pants looked funny all droopy and full of water.

Jonas had to take off all his clothes, and Mother hung them up in a tree to dry. But the clothes were still not dry when we were ready

to leave. So Jonas had to sit in the car wrapped in a blanket.

Lotta thought that was funny, too. But suddenly she stopped laughing. She couldn't find Bamsie. We looked everywhere. But Bamsie was gone. Mother said that we would have to leave without him, and that made Lotta scream louder than when Jonas fell into the lake.

"Bamsie can have a wonderful night in the

woods all by himself," Daddy said. "Tomorrow I'll come back and try to find him."

This made Lotta cry and cry. "Maybe a wicked old witch will come and frighten him," she said.

"If Bamsie meets a witch it will probably be the witch who gets the biggest scare," said Daddy.

"Can you remember when you last had Bamsie?" Mother asked.

Lotta tried to think. "Twelve o'clock," she said.

But since Lotta can't tell time that was just a big lie.

Daddy says that Lotta is a tough little nut who says anything that comes into her head.

Suddenly I remembered that Lotta had Bamsie when we were looking at the bird's nest. We all went back to the tree and there, right beside the bird's nest, sat Bamsie! Lotta picked him up and kissed him on his snout and said:

"Darling Bamsie, have you been sitting here

the whole time looking at those little blue eggs?"

"The poor mother bird probably hasn't dared come back to her eggs all day," said Jonas. "Piggly bears make the best scarecrows."

"Bamsie hasn't touched a thing," Lotta said. "He's only been sitting here looking at the eggs."

We all got in the car and drove home. Jonas had to sit wrapped up in a blanket all the way.

That night Mother and Daddy came to our room to say good night as they always do. Daddy stooped down next to Lotta's bed. She lay there with her dirty Bamsie beside her.

Daddy said, "Well, Little Nut, what did you enjoy most today? I'll bet it was when you found Bamsie."

"No, the best part was when Jonas fell in the lake," said Lotta.

We Visit Our Grandparents

In the summertime we go with Mother to visit our grandparents in the country. Daddy comes when he gets his vacation. We go by train because Mother can't drive the car.

"Be good on the train and don't make it too hard for your mother," said Daddy as we got on board.

"Do we only have to be good on the train?" Jonas shouted.

"No, everywhere," said Daddy.

"But you said that we only had to be good on the train," Lotta said.

The train started to move, and all Daddy could do was wave to us. We waved back and shouted good-by.

We went along the corridor of the train and into our compartment. We were alone there except for an old man who squeezed in. Lotta had her Bamsie and I had my biggest doll whose name is Maud Yvonne Marlene.

The old gentleman had a wart on his chin, and when he got up to stand by the window, out in the corridor, Lotta said to Mother in a loud whisper:

"That old man has a wart on his chin. . . ."

"Hush," said Mother. "He can hear you."

Lotta looked surprised and said, "Doesn't he know that he has a wart on his chin?"

The conductor came to collect the tickets.

Only Mother and Jonas had tickets because
Lotta and I still ride for half fare.

"How old is this little girl?" the conductor
asked, pointing to me. I said that I would soon
be six.

He didn't ask how old Lotta was because he
could see that she was too small to need any
ticket.

But Lotta told him, "I'm four years old

and Mother is thirty-two. And this is Bamsie."

Then the conductor laughed and said that on this train all Bamsies could ride free.

In the beginning we sat very still and looked out the window. But soon we got tired of that. So Jonas and I went out into the corridor and into the other compartments and talked to people. Now and then we came back to see Mother so she wouldn't worry. Mother was busy telling Lotta one story after another so that Lotta would sit still. She didn't want Lotta to go out into the corridor because you never know what Lotta will do next.

"Now tell me about the two goats or I'll go out in the corridor," Lotta said, when Mother had finished a story.

At lunchtime we ate sandwiches and drank soda. Lotta took a piece of salami from her sandwich and stuck it on the window. Mother got very angry with her.

"Lotta, why do you smear the salami on the window?"

49

"Because it sticks much better than the meatballs," said Lotta.

Then Mother really got angry at her. Mother had to rub the train window with paper napkins for a long time before it got clean.

Once when the train stopped at a station, Jonas decided that he and I should get off for a breath of fresh air. We couldn't get the door open but a lady helped us.

"Are you getting off at this station?" she asked.

"Yes," we said.

We were getting off but we were getting back on, of course.

We stepped off the train and went all the way back to the last car and got on again. Then we walked back through the whole train until we

came to our own compartment. Mother and the lady who had helped us with the door were talking to the conductor. Mother was crying. "But you must stop the train. My children got off!" she said.

"But we got back on again!" Jonas shouted as we ran up to them.

Then Mother began to cry again, and the lady who had helped us open the door scolded us. I could never understand why that lady scolded us when she was the one who had helped us get out of the train.

"Now, you just go and sit down in that compartment and don't you move," Mother said.

But there was no Lotta in the compartment. "Where's Lotta?" I asked. And Mother almost started to cry again.

We finally found Lotta in a compartment much farther down. She was busy telling a story to a lot of people. As we arrived we heard her saying:

"In our compartment there is a man who has

a wart on his chin but he doesn't know about it."

Mother grabbed Lotta and pulled her back to our own compartment. After that we had to sit there without moving because Mother was very, very angry and said that it would be easier to watch a herd of wild buffalo than to try to keep track of us.

Buffalo reminded me that I would see baby calves at my grandparents', and that made me very happy. When we got to the station we took a taxi out to our grandparents' house.

They were standing on the front porch waving. Their dog, Lucas, was barking and jumping up and down. The whole place smelled of summer.

"Welcome, my little darlings," said Grandmother.

"Some darlings!" Mother mumbled.

"Tomorrow we may ride Blackie," said Grandfather.

"Come to the barn and I'll show you Muriel's kittens," said Grandmother.

"Do you have any candy left in your cupboard?" Lotta asked.

"Let's have a look," Grandmother said. "I just might have some left."

Then we knew that we had come back home to Grandmother and Grandfather.

Lotta Almost Curses

In our grandparents' garden there is a big tree
with a real tree house up in the branches! There
is a ladder leading up to a sort of platform with a
table and benches and a fence around it to keep
us from falling down. Grandmother calls it the
Green Pavilion. I like eating in trees better than
anywhere else.

When we woke up the first morning, the first thing Jonas said was, "Grandmother, let's eat all our meals in the Green Pavilion!"

"And what do you think Klara would say if she had to drag food up that rickety ladder three times a day?"

Klara is Grandmother's maid. She is very nice but she doesn't like to eat in trees. "I would say No," Klara said.

"But, Grandmother, we can carry our food up to the Green Pavilion ourselves," I said.

"If you don't let us, we'll be very angry," said Lotta.

Grandmother said she wouldn't want her Lotta to be angry, and so she made a whole pile of pancakes and packed them in a basket together with a bag of sugar and small jar of jam. She also packed some plates and forks, three cups and a bottle of milk.

Then we went off to the Green Pavilion. Jonas climbed up first. I followed him and then came Lotta.

"I would really laugh if you dropped the basket, Jonas," Lotta said.

But Jonas didn't drop the basket. We unpacked everything on the table and sat down on the benches. We ate our pancakes with jam and sugar. There were such a lot of pancakes that even Lotta couldn't eat them all. You know what she did with them? She hung them on the tree!

"I'm pretending they are leaves," she said.

The pancakes waved in the wind and they did look almost like leaves.

"If Mother finds out about this you'll get it," I said.

But Lotta didn't care about what I said. She just sat there looking at her pancakes. She sang a song that Daddy sometimes sings. It begins like this:

"The wind rustles the leaves, tra-la . . ."

After a while Lotta got hungry again and took bites out of all the hanging pancakes.

"I'm pretending that I'm a little lamb, nibbling at leaves in the woods," she said.

A bird flew by and Lotta said to him, "You may nibble at my pancakes, but not Jonas and Mia Maria."

The bird didn't want any pancakes. But Jonas
and I were hungry again. I stretched out my
hand to Lotta and said, "Please give a poor
beggar something to eat."

60

Lotta gave me a pancake that she had taken a bite out of. I put sugar and jam on it and it tasted very good even though it was only a half a pancake. Jonas got pancakes from Lotta, too.

"Please give a poor beggar something to eat," he said.

Lotta likes anything that is silly. Finally, when we had eaten up all of Lotta's pancakes, she said, "The pancake leaves are all gone. Now you have to start eating the green ones!"

She ripped off a whole handful of green leaves and wanted us to eat them. But Jonas and I said that we weren't hungry any more.

"They taste all right if you put sugar and jam on them," Lotta told us, and she put some jam and sugar on a green leaf and ate it.

"You'd better make sure there is no worm on that leaf," Jonas said.

"The worm has to watch out for himself," said Lotta.

"That kid has an answer for everything," as Grandfather would say.

The following day, which happened to be a Sunday, we had fried fish for lunch and, next to salmon patties, it's the worst thing Lotta knows. When the weather is pleasant, Grandmother and Grandfather always eat at a table that stands under the biggest tree in the garden. Grandfather, Grandmother, Mother, Jonas, and I were all sitting around the table ready to eat, but Lotta kept on playing with the cat. She wouldn't come even though Mother called her several times. Finally, she came and when she saw that we were having fish, she said:

"Fish on Sunday! Damn it!"

Mother got very angry with her because she had told Lotta a thousand times not to say "damn," which is almost a swearword. Mother warned Lotta that if she said "damn" once more she wouldn't be allowed to stay in the country with Grandmother but would have to go back to town.

Lotta wasn't allowed to sit at the table with us because she had said that bad word. And while

we were eating our lunch, Lotta walked around the garden crying.

When we had finished, she had to eat alone at the table. She howled and howled. Mother told Jonas and me to run along and play because Lotta had to be alone until she was good again. But we hid behind the corner of the house and watched Lotta cry. At last she quieted down, but that was only because she had another one of her ideas. She picked up the fish on her plate and walked over to the rain barrel that was standing under the drain spout. Lotta dropped the fish into it. But Mother had been watching Lotta too.

"He needs to swim a little—damn it!"

"Lotta, remember what I told you," Mother warned.

Lotta nodded and ran into the house. After a few minutes she came back carrying her own little suitcase. A belt hung outside the bag and trailed behind her when she walked. Mother, Grandmother, Grandfather, Jonas, and I watched her. Lotta was about to leave. She went up to Grandmother and Grandfather, curtsied politely and said, "I am going home to Daddy because he is much nicer than Mother."

She didn't say good-by to Mother or Jonas or me. We watched her as she walked off with the belt still dragging behind her. When she reached the gate she stopped and just stood there for a long time not moving. Finally, Mother went to her and said, "Well, Lotta, aren't you going to leave?"

"I can't ride alone on the train, damn it," Lotta said.

Then Mother picked up Lotta in her arms and said that she had better stay because it would be so sad for everyone if she left. Lotta threw her arms around Mother's neck, and sobbed. She wouldn't talk to Jonas and me even when we tried to be nice to her.

That night when we had gone to bed, Grandmother came into our room and told us stories from the Bible. She showed us pictures from it,

65

and one was of a boy named Joseph. Grandmother said that Pharaoh, the king of Egypt, gave Joseph a beautiful ring.

Suddenly Lotta said: "1, 2, 3, 4, 5, Grandmother, what did you say?"

Since Lotta's learned to count she hardly ever says "damn" any more.

Lotta's Unlucky Day

One of our favorite places at our grandparents' is the doll house. It belonged to Mother and Aunt Katie when they were little girls. Their dolls live in that house. It is painted red and is tucked away in a corner of the garden with a small path leading up to it. It has a little lawn all its own where daisies grow. The doll house is furnished with white tables and chairs, and there is a closet with dolls' dishes, a frying pan and an iron and a small jug with matching glasses for juice. There is also a little chair which was Grandmother's when she was a girl. It's hard to believe that a chair could be that old!

One day when we played there, we pretended that Jonas was Daddy, and I was Mother, and Lotta was Klara, our maid.

"Now Daddy is going to take the baby out," said Jonas. He took the doll carriage with Aunt Katie's doll and went out into the garden.

"And I'm going to scrub the kitchen floor," Lotta said.

"No, first of all we're going to make cheese," I said. Since I was the mother, I was going to make the decisions.

"No cheese before I've scrubbed the floor," Lotta said.

Jonas told Lotta that she couldn't play with us if she didn't do what we told her to. So we made cheese. When you make cheese you take berries and put them in a handkerchief. Then you squeeze out all the juice, and what is left in the handkerchief you make into small round cheeses that are very sour.

"*Now* I'm going to scrub the floor," Lotta said.

She picked up the pail and went into Grandmother's kitchen to get some water. When she came back she emptied the whole bucket on the doll-house floor. Then she got down on her knees and began to scrub with a soapy brush. She got herself very wet.

"Are you swimming or what are you doing?"

asked Jonas, who had just come in with the baby.

"I'm scrubbing the floor because the floor has to be scrubbed," Lotta said. "Besides, that's the most fun."

Lotta finished her scrubbing very quickly. "That's done," she said. And Jonas and I had to mop up the water. Lotta didn't help at all. She just stood around watching us.

The *real* Klara is always singing and dancing in the kitchen. Sometimes she does a little jig and sings:

Tra la la! Yo-ho-ho!
When I dance I think about you.

Now Lotta was doing exactly what Klara did.
She was dancing around, singing, "Tra la la!
Yo-ho-ho! When I dance I think about you!"
The only difference was that she took the egg
beater that hangs on the wall in the doll house,
dipped it into the pail, and sprayed water all
over Jonas and me. Then she laughed as hard as

she could. We got very angry with her and told her if she was going to be that silly she could mop up the water herself. But Lotta just kept on dancing and splashing water around. The floor was slippery from all the soap, and suddenly Lotta fell and hit her head on the cupboard. Poor Lotta.

"It's no fun being Klara!" she cried.

After that she went outside to find the cat, and left Jonas and me to play by ourselves. We made spinach from lilac leaves and ate cheese and spinach—we only made believe, of course.

All of a sudden we heard Lotta scream, and when we looked out she was pulling the cat by the tail. The cat was yowling and scratching at her.

"All I did was hold him by the stem, and he got angry and scratched me!" she cried.

Mother and Grandmother had gone out, so we went to look for Klara to give us a Band-Aid for Lotta's scratches. Klara wasn't in the kitchen. Lotta had forgotten to turn off the

faucet when she got the water to scrub the floor, and I can tell you that there was ten times more water on the kitchen floor than there was in the doll house when Lotta was scrubbing. Jonas sloshed through the water and turned off the tap. Just then Klara came in.

"Jonas, what on earth are you doing?" she cried, wringing her hands.

"He is swimming." Lotta laughed. Next, Klara wanted to know who had forgotten to turn off the faucet.

"I did," said Lotta.

"But why would you forget to do a thing like that?" Klara asked her.

Lotta sighed, and said, "Because this is my unlucky day."

74

It seems to me that Lotta has an unlucky day almost every day.

Klara mopped up the floor and put a Band-Aid on Lotta. Then she served us hot chocolate and buns at the kitchen table. While she was doing this, she danced around and sang:

Tra la la! Yo-ho-ho!
When I dance I think about you.

Lotta ate five buns, Jonas ate four, and I ate three.

"This is a very nice unlucky day," Lotta said, and she gave Klara a big hug.

Klara said that Lotta was a nice little kid, after all.

Lotta in Jail

Jonas, Lotta, and I have two cousins. They belong to our Aunt Katie. Last summer while we were in the country, Aunt Katie came to visit, and she brought her children with her. Their names are Anna Jo and Thomas. Anna Jo is as old as Jonas. Thomas is as old as Lotta. Anna Jo can get the better of Jonas in a fight because she is very strong and very determined.

Lotta can beat Thomas without even trying, although Mother has forbidden her to fight.

"Why do you hit Thomas?" Mother always asks Lotta.

Then Lotta says, "Because he is so nice when he cries."

One time Mother made Lotta sit in the doll house all by herself for hitting Thomas. Then Anna Jo had a bright idea.

"Let's pretend that Lotta is in jail and that we are going to rescue her," she said.

"First we have to smuggle in some food to her. In jails they only give you bread and water."

We went to the kitchen and asked Klara for some cold meatballs. Anna Jo put them in a little basket that we use when we go berrying. Then Jonas and Anna Jo climbed up on the roof of the doll house and called down to Lotta. They told her that she was a convict in jail and that we were sending some food down to her through the chimney. Lotta stuck her head out the window and asked them why she couldn't get her food through the window or the door.

"Isn't the door locked?" Anna Jo asked.

"No, this jail is no good," Lotta said. "Come to the door and give me the meatballs."

Anna Jo got very angry and said that when you were in jail you had to have the food sent down through the chimney. "And that's that," said Anna Jo.

Then Lotta had to give in.

Anna Jo tied a long string to the basket and lowered it down the chimney. She let Jonas help a little, but Thomas and I had to stand down below and watch.

"Here come the meatballs," Lotta called from inside the doll house, "and lots of soot, too," she said.

Thomas and I peeked through the window and watched Lotta wolf down all the meatballs. They were covered with soot, and Lotta's face and hands got all dirty. Anna Jo was very pleased when she saw Lotta's sooty

face. Now Lotta really looked like a bad criminal. Thomas started to cry because he knew that criminals were dangerous.

"Silly, she's not really a criminal. She's Lotta."

"But she looks mean and dangerous," Thomas cried.

Lotta liked to see Thomas cry, so she made faces at him through the window. Then she said, "I *might* be a dangerous criminal, Thomas." She looked at Jonas and me and said, "Help me get out right away because I want to go around frightening people. I like it when people are afraid of me!"

Anna Jo and Jonas went around to the back of the house to rescue Lotta through the window. We got our teeter-totter because Anna Jo said that we could use it for a bridge over the deep ditch that was supposed to surround the jail. We put the board against the window and Anna Jo and Jonas and I climbed in the window to rescue Lotta. Thomas stood outside, watching and crying.

When we got inside the doll house Lotta wasn't there. Anna Jo was furious.

"Now, where has that brat gone?" she screamed.

"I've escaped," said Lotta when we finally found her. She was sitting in the currant bushes just stuffing herself with bright red currants.

"But we were going to rescue you," Anna Jo said.

"I rescued myself," Lotta told her.

"You're just impossible to play with," Jonas told her.

"Ha, ha," said Lotta.

Then Mother came and saw that Lotta wasn't sitting in the doll house.

"Are you good now?" Mother called.

"Yes, but I am all *dirty*." Lotta pointed to her face, and Mother clapped her hands and exclaimed, "My goodness, just look at you!"

Lotta was sent out to the laundry and had to scrub at herself with soap for a whole half hour. That afternoon we took the meatball basket and went off to pick wild strawberries. There are lots of them in the fields. While we were berrying we saw a snake. Everyone screamed and was terrified—everyone, that is, except Thomas.

"Look, there is a tail without its doggie," he said. He didn't even know what a snake was.

When we got home we divided the wild strawberries so that we all had the same amount. But Anna Jo got the biggest and the reddest.

Thomas and Lotta sat down on the veranda to eat their berries. All of a sudden Thomas began to cry. Aunt Katie stuck her head out of the window and asked: "Why is Thomas crying?"

"He's crying because I won't let him eat my berries," said Lotta.

"Has he finished his?" Aunt Katie asked.

"Yes," said Lotta. "They are all gone. And he cried while I was eating them, too."

Then Mother came out. She took Lotta's berries and gave them to Thomas.

"I think I'll go to bed," Lotta said.

"I think you'd better," Mother said. "You are very tired."

"No, I'm not," Lotta said. "My legs won't stop moving. But I'll go to bed anyway!"

That night Lotta was nice to Thomas. He was supposed to sleep in the small guest room by himself, but he was afraid of the dark and cried and wanted the door left open.

"But, Thomas, dear, you're never afraid of the dark when you're at home," Aunt Katie said.

"At home it's his own dark, Aunt Katie. He isn't used to Grandmother's dark," Lotta said.

Thomas was allowed to sleep in our room.

Lotta kissed him and tucked him in and said:

"Now I'll sing to you, Thomas, and you won't be afraid any more."

Lotta sang the lullaby Mother always sings to us:

> *God's little angels,*
> *Spread out your wings*
> *And watch our children*
> *'Til night has flown by . . .*

"And Lotta, too," said Lotta.

Christmastime Is Wonderful

One day Jonas asked me:

"Which do you like best—the sun, the moon, or the stars?"

I said that I liked them all, but maybe the stars just a little bit more because they shine so beautifully on Christmas night, and I love Christmas so much!

I was hoping to get skis for Christmas and I was afraid that there wouldn't be any snow. Lotta wanted it to snow because she wanted to sled. One night just before Christmas, when we were in bed, Lotta said:

"I've asked Daddy for a sled but now I have to ask God for snow, otherwise I can't use it."

"Dear God, let it snow right away," she prayed. "Think of the poor flowers. They need a warm blanket to cover them while they are sleeping in the cold ground."

Then she looked up over the edge of her bed and whispered to me:

"This time I was clever. I didn't tell him that the snow was for my sled!"

Imagine how excited we were the next morning when we woke up and saw that it was snowing! Jonas and Lotta and I stood at the window in our pajamas and watched the snowflakes settling in our garden—and in Mrs. Berg's garden, too.

We dressed as fast as we could and went out.

Then we had a snowball fight and made a beautiful snowman, and when Daddy came home he put his hat on it.

88

We had fun all day, and Mother was glad to have us out of the way because Mrs. Fransson was helping her with the Christmas house-cleaning. Lotta likes to talk to Mrs. Fransson. She calls her "Fransson," but Mother tells her that she has to say "Mrs." Fransson. Mrs. Fransson also likes to talk to Lotta, but Mother has told her not to answer when Lotta calls her "Fransson."

During lunch the day we made the snowman Lotta said to Mrs. Fransson:

"Fransson, feel how wet my gloves are!"

Mrs. Fransson didn't answer her, and Lotta said: "Fransson, have you seen our snowman?"

But Mrs. Fransson still didn't answer.

Lotta was quiet for a long time and then she said:

"Damn it, why are you mad at me, Fransson?"

Then Mother said: "Lotta, you know that you're not allowed to say 'damn,' and besides, you must say 'Mrs.' Fransson."

"Then I won't be able to talk to her at all," Lotta said.

Mrs. Fransson told Lotta that she liked to talk to her very much and asked Mother to let Lotta call her "Fransson." Then Mother laughed and said that it was all right.

"And 'damn,' too?" asked Lotta.

"No, not 'damn,'" said Mother.

When Mother left, Lotta said:

"I know what I'll do. When I mean 'damn' I'll say 'Fransson,' because Mother let's me say 'Fransson' now."

"Fransson, what fun Christmas is!"

And it really is, fun I mean. Jonas and I and Lotta helped Mother to get everything ready for Christmas. We shoveled snow in the yard and put up a Christmas shelf for the birds. Mother said that we were very helpful.

"I don't know what I would do without you," she said.

Lotta, who was wiping the knives very carefully, said:

"I don't know what I would do if I didn't have me. But, oh, Fransson, how I have to slave!"

Buying Christmas presents is great fun, too. It's exciting to go shopping when there is snow on the ground. The market place is full of Christmas trees, and people are rushing in and out of stores.

One day we took our piggy banks that we had been stuffing all year and went in town to buy Christmas presents. Jonas and I wanted to get a small doll for Lotta to play with in her bath, so we told her to wait for us in the street while we went into the toy store.

"But you musn't peek," Jonas said.

"Go and look in the window of the pastry shop next door," I told her.

Lotta was delighted because there were so many candy pigs and other wonderful goodies in Karlman's window.

When Jonas and I came out of the toy shop, Lotta had disappeared. We looked up and down,

and then we saw her coming out of Karlman's.

"What did you do?" Jonas asked her.

"I bought you a Christmas present," Lotta said.

"What did you buy?" Jonas wanted to know.

"A creampuff," Lotta said.

"How stupid can you be?" Jonas said. "That won't last until Christmas!"

"I knew that," Lotta said, "so I ate it."

Then we saw our daddy walking along the street. He didn't know that we were in town alone doing our Christmas shopping.

"It seems to me that I've seen these children somewhere before," Daddy said. "They look so nice I think I'll give them a treat."

We jumped up and down with excitement. Daddy let us drink all the hot chocolate and eat all the pastry we wanted. We sat in the green booth at Karlman's, watching all the people with their Christmas packages. Outside, the snow was settling on the street, and our cream-puffs had lots of cream in them. A lady whose name was Mrs. Friberg came up to us and began talking to Daddy. Jonas and I sat and listened. But Lotta was babbling away even more than Mrs. Friberg. Finally, Daddy said:

"Lotta, you are not supposed to interrupt grownups when they are talking. Please keep

93

still. You should wait until we are finished."

"Oh," said Lotta, "I've tried, but it doesn't work because they just never stop."

Then Mrs. Friberg laughed and said that she had to go home to make gingerbread men.

The following day we also made gingerbread men—all by ourselves. We made so many that Jonas and Lotta and I each had a jarful. We kept them in our room. We were planning to save them until Christmas. But Lotta finished hers the same day and then, of course, couldn't eat her dinner.

"I ate them because they might not last until Christmas Eve," she said.

Every day she came begging Jonas and me to share ours.

"Give a poor beggar something to eat," she said.

At last it was Christmas Eve, and that is the most wonderful day of the whole year.

As soon as we woke up, we ran down to the kitchen. Mother was there, making coffee.

Then we all sat in front of the fire in the living room having breakfast, and stuffing ourselves with saffron buns, gingerbread, and pastry. The Christmas tree filled the room with such a wonderful smell. After breakfast we trimmed the tree, Daddy, Jonas, Lotta, and I. Mother was in the kitchen making lunch.

"Our house is so beautiful," said Jonas. "I think it's the most beautiful house in town."

"And it has the best smells," Lotta chimed in.

Mother had potted hyacinths that smelled very good, and everywhere there were candles that looked and smelled different from the way candles usually smell. I like Christmas to smell different from any other day.

We kept eating all day long and we dunked bread in a huge pot of broth on the stove, which is a tradition with us at Christmastime. That afternoon Mother visited Mrs. Berg and gave her some Christmas presents and Mrs. Berg gave Mother some candy and burnt almonds. Mrs. Berg also gave Lotta a pretty red cap that she had knitted herself.

"If I put this on, I can almost be a Santa Claus," Lotta said.

That night the real Santa Claus came. He stamped his feet outside, banged on the door,

and came in with a sack on his back that was filled to the brim with Christmas presents.

"I don't have to ask if there are any good children here, because I see that there are," he said. Then he turned to Lotta: "Now, don't let those eyes roll out of your head!"

But Lotta stood there and stared at him with big round eyes.

Santa Claus went outside and came back with

two huge packages. One contained my skis and the other was Lotta's sled. But Lotta stood there not moving until Santa Claus had gone.

"Why are you so quiet, Lotta?" Mother asked.

"Because it tickles in my stomach when I see Santa Claus," Lotta said. "Fransson, how my stomach tickles!"

That night we were allowed to stay up as late as we wanted to. We cracked nuts and ate oranges in front of the fireplace and danced around the Christmas tree. Everything was so wonderful.

The next day, Christmas morning, we got up very, very early to go to church. The shelf that we had set out for the birds was covered with snow. We brushed it off so that the sparrows would be able to eat. It was so early that the stars were still out. That's why I love the stars most of all. When the stars shine over Troublemaker Street everything looks so unreal. Most of the houses are brightly lit, and above the Town

Hall roof a single star glitters—the biggest star
I've ever seen.

"It's probably the Christmas star," says Lotta.